WARNING!

Scaredy Squirrel insists that everyone avoid reading this Safety Guide during a full moon.

Mélanie Watt

Scaredy Squirrel

prepares for
HALLOWEEN

KIDS CAN PRESS

MÉLANIE WATT PRODUCTIONS

This **Safety Guide** must never be handled by:

- sticky fingers

- claws

- tentacles

Please note that this book is not meant to travel:

A. through walls

B. by broom

C. by dragon

CONTENTS

PREFACE

CHAPTER 1
HALLOWEEN IS COMING

CHAPTER 2
HALLOWEEN DECORATIONS

CHAPTER 3
HALLOWEEN COSTUMES

SCAREDY SQUIRREL
IN A NUTSHELL

IDENTIFICATION FORM

Name: _SCAREDY ORVILLE SQUIRREL_

Initials: _S.O.S._

Born: _OCTOBER 3RD_

at: _13:28 HOURS AND 6 SECONDS_ in _NUT TREE_.

Likes: _LISTS, PLANS AND SAFETY EQUIPMENT_

Dislikes: _DANGER AND UNPREDICTABILITY_

Pet peeves: _GERMS IN GENERAL_

Hard hat
(a solid ally)

Nut tree

Rubber gloves
(a germ barrier)

Folder
(an organizer's dream)

THE SCAREDY

1. Halloween makes me ...

smile ☐ (0 points)

grin ☐ (0 points)

pass out ☐ (1 point)

2. Pumpkins are best used for ...

jack-o'-lanterns ☐ (0 points)

smashing ☐ (0 points)

a great source of fiber ☐ (1 point)

3. Halloween decorations can be ...

whimsical ☐ (0 points)

magical ☐ (0 points)

nerve-wracking ☐ (1 point)

4. RIP stands for ...

Rest in Peace ☐ (0 points)

React in Panic ☐ (1 point)

HALLOWEEN QUIZ

5. On Halloween, spiderwebs should be ...

everywhere ☐ (0 points)

vacuumed ☐ (1 point)

6. Haunted houses are ...

a lot of fun ☐ (0 points)

entertaining ☐ (0 points)

not-to-code major danger hazards ☐ (1 point)

7. Trick or treat, smell my feet ...

give me something good to eat ☐ (0 points)

give me something to floss my teeth ☐ (1 point)

8. What do you see?

a friendly fruit bat ☐ (0 points)

a thirsty vampire on a quest to bite everything in its path and take over the universe with a vengeance ☐ (1 point)

IMPORTANT!
If, like Scaredy, your total points range between
1 and 8, this Safety Guide was made for you!

ABOUT THIS SAFETY GUIDE

Salutations, ghostly readers.
Halloween is creeping up quickly,
and it's time to gather the courage
to face the ghoulish festivities!

Which is why I, Scaredy Squirrel,
have created this essential Safety Guide.

Divided into eight spellbinding chapters, this
book is designed to help you prepare for and
survive Halloween, all in one piece!

Now, let's begin!

S.O.S.

fake

500 thread count,
ironed sheets

battery
operated

candelabra extinguisher
(just in case)

Scaredy
Squirrel
prepares for
HALLOWEEN

A SAFETY GUIDE FOR SCAREDIES

CHAPTER 1

HALLOWEEN
IS COMING

SECURING THE AREA
It's crucial to secure your living area in time for Halloween by using the items below:

garlic

scarecrow

blender

bug repellent

caution tape

doghouse

THE DANGER-PROOF PLAN

A blender on HIGH makes a deafening noise sure to keep ghosts and goblins away!

Black cats and witches will be shaking in their boots when they spot this scarecrow!

Beware, werewolves! This vacant doghouse gives the illusion that your home is well guarded.

Living area is here.

Repel creepy crawlers by spraying the area!

Garnish with garlic to stink out vampires!

Secure perimeter with caution tape!

A SCAREDY TIP!

Vampires, ghosts and witches are in fact fictional, but a squirrel can never be too careful!

CHAPTER 2

HALLOWEEN
DECORATIONS

SAFELY CARVING A JACK-O'-LANTERN

Halloween jitters are an oh-so-common reality. Carving a jack-o'-lantern can be a shaky experience, especially when you're not your usual stable self!

NOT OKAY TO HANDLE:

chainsaw

ax

peeler

fire

OKAY TO HANDLE:

plastic knife

rubber spatula

wooden spoon

flashlight

NOTICE!

When carving a facial expression, always go with a friendly look:

STEP-BY-STEP CARVING INSTRUCTIONS

1. Select a pumpkin with the perfect orange color.

2. Carve a perfect circle on top of pumpkin.

3. Scrape seeds with spatula, then remove with wooden spoon.

4. Draw face on photogenic side of pumpkin.

5. Delicately carve friendly features.

6. Insert flashlight, position lid and congratulate yourself!

CURB APPEAL

Decorating your doorway is the neighborly thing to do. It shows trick-or-treaters whether you are home or not and sends out an inviting message.

NOT INVITING

INVITING

HAPPY NON-THREATENING HALLOWEEN!

DO NOT DISTURB

WELCOME!

A SCAREDY TIP!

Around Halloween, if you're the courageous type, resist the urge to vacuum every minute. Soon your decor will look like the inside of a dusty manor in Transylvania.

MULTITASKING: SOUND EFFECTS 101

Think outside the coffin box! Add spooky sound effects and get important chores done at the same time!

kaboom! kaboom!

Start a load of laundry.

spluurch! spluurch!

Chew with your mouth open.

screech! screech!

Write lists on a chalkboard.

A GHOULISH INTERIOR
(BUT NOT TOO GHOULISH)

Decorate your living room without making it look too scary.
Going overboard could freak you out!

BROOM
A bewitching effect.
Sweep up
dust bunnies
when nobody
is looking!

SOCK
There's nothing worse
than a lost sock to
reek havoc!

CRYSTAL BALL
A mystical addition
that guests
could not have
predicted!

SHEETS
They transform your
room into a ghostly
retreat and protect
your furniture!

**EMPTY
HAND SANITIZER
BOTTLE**
Hands down the most
terrifying scenario!
But obviously, you have
backups stashed away.

OLD TELEVISION
Turn on a channel with
lots of static for
something much scarier
than a horror movie!

A SCAREDY TIP!
Need more pizzazz?
Use the traditional Halloween color
scheme, and as a bonus,
eliminate the scare factor ...

A few unscary **BLACk** items to decorate with:

top hats	Black Forest cakes	umbrellas
bowling balls	pianos	bow ties

A few unscary ORANGE items to decorate with:

| popsicles | safety cones | carrots |
| hard hats | golf balls | flotation vests |

CHAPTER 3

HALLOWEEN COSTUMES

HALLOWEEN COSTUMES
(SO MANY CHOICES, SO LITTLE TIME!)

Picking a Halloween costume is no easy task.
Start evaluating your options in early June.
Because there's such a wide range to choose from,
here are a few themes to get your
beetle juices flowing!

NOTICE! A handy SCARE-O-METER is graciously provided
by Scaredy Squirrel to help you gauge the fear factor.

A SCAREDY TIP!
The outdoors can send chills down
your spine. So cover up by layering several
costumes. Peel off the layers as the night
unfolds and bedazzle your friends!

THEME: CLASSICS

ZOMBIE

BRIDE OF FRANKENSTEIN

WEREWOLF

UNSCARY · SCARY · TERRIFYING

UNSCARY · SCARY · TERRIFYING

UNSCARY · SCARY · TERRIFYING

GHOST

VAMPIRE

WITCH

UNSCARY · SCARY · TERRIFYING

UNSCARY · SCARY · TERRIFYING

UNSCARY · SCARY · TERRIFYING

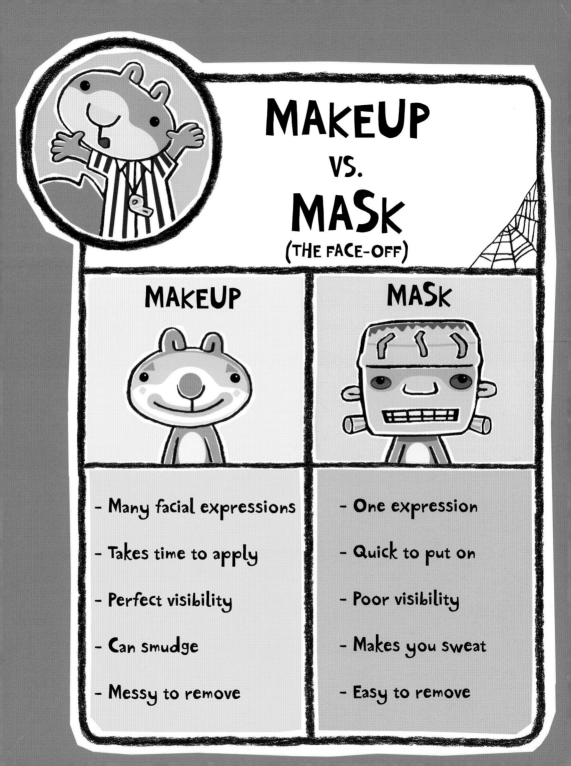

DO-IT-YOURSELF PROJECTS

With a little brainstorming, your Halloween costume can become a work of art! Use common items found in every home to construct a truly unique masterpiece that will be all the rage!

*Duct tape not included

TO MAKE A **MUMMY** COSTUME

JUST GATHER:

DRAMATIZATION

6 ½ rolls of extra-soft two-ply toilet paper

WEATHER WARNING! Whatever you do, do not go out in the rain.

CHAPTER 4

HALLOWEEN
TRICK-OR-TREATING

THE TRICK-OR-TREATING MAP

Crossing the street for candy is risky business, especially with all the spooky obstacles Halloween can attract!

URBAN LEGEND

- STOP
- CHICKENS
- UFOs
- HAUNTED MANSIONS
- CAULDRONS
- SEA MONSTERS
- LADDERS
- BLACK CATS
- CARNIVOROUS PLANTS

Cauldrons spell trouble. Someone's cooking up a storm, so hurry!

Watch out! Unidentified Flying Objects will beam you up in the blink of an eyeball!

LET'S SAY I AM HERE.

CHAPTER 5

HALLOWEEN
CANDY

GETTING TO KNOW YOUR HALLOWEEN CANDY

Here are a few tasty sweets you might gather while trick-or-treating.
But before you devour anything, remember ...

CHOCOLATE

PROS: Rich and milky

CONS: Melts in your paw and could attract bunnies

HARD CANDY

PROS: Nice sugary crunch

CONS: Could break a tooth

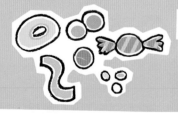

SOUR CANDY

PROS: Awakens taste buds

CONS: Causes silly faces

JELLY CANDY

PROS: Refreshing fruity taste

CONS: No vitamins

GUM

PROS: Helps digestion

CONS: Loud chewing noises
and sudden pops

OTHER

PROS: Healthier than candy

CONS: It's NOT candy

A SCAREDY TIP!
Schedule a visit to the dentist for
early the next morning, and your
teeth will thank you for it!

CANDY TRANSPORTATION

Plan your strategy according to your experience
and the length of your trick-or-treating route.

AMATEUR

Route length: 1 apartment

Load size: little bit of candy

BEGINNER

Route length: 10 houses

Load size: bucket of candy

ADVANCED

Route length: 1 block

Load size: pile of candy

HAPPY HALLOWEEN!

PROFESSIONAL

Route length: 1 neighborhood

Load size: ton of candy

A SCAREDY TIP!

Getting in great physical shape before
Halloween is a must. Being fit and strong
helps you carry the weight!

DETECTING QUALITY

Before attempting to eat a treat, you must hand it over for thorough inspection. Ask a parent or loved one with experience in food quality control to give you their stamp of approval!

A FEW EXAMPLES THAT DO NOT PASS INSPECTION:

half-eaten candy

toad stuck to candy

expired candy

someone else's candy

CHAPTER 6

HALLOWEEN NOTES

Here are a few notes everyone needs to read before kick-starting Halloween:

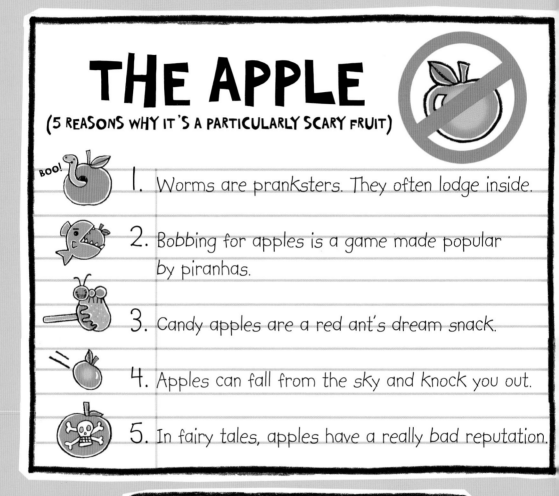

THE APPLE
(5 REASONS WHY IT'S A PARTICULARLY SCARY FRUIT)

1. Worms are pranksters. They often lodge inside.

2. Bobbing for apples is a game made popular by piranhas.

3. Candy apples are a red ant's dream snack.

4. Apples can fall from the sky and knock you out.

5. In fairy tales, apples have a really bad reputation.

A SCAREDY TIP!
The more you know about infamous Halloween monsters, the bigger your chances of outwitting them.

CHAPTER 7

HALLOWEEN
FUN

PARTY PLANNING

Making rules is an important part of entertaining.
Don't let things get out of control!
Prepare an agreement for your guests to sign.

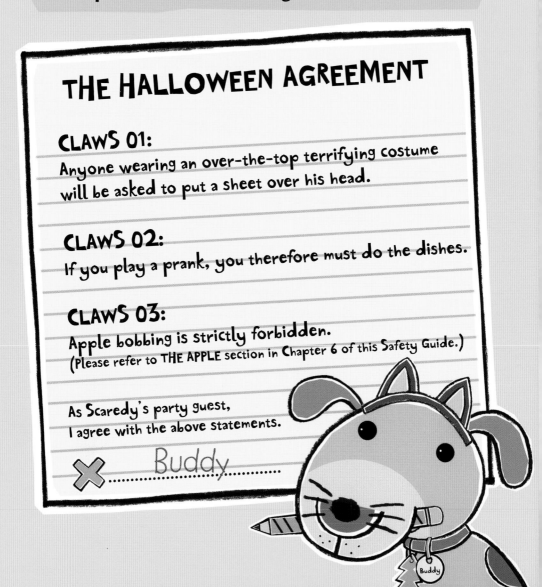

THE HALLOWEEN AGREEMENT

CLAWS 01:
Anyone wearing an over-the-top terrifying costume
will be asked to put a sheet over his head.

CLAWS 02:
If you play a prank, you therefore must do the dishes.

CLAWS 03:
Apple bobbing is strictly forbidden.
(Please refer to THE APPLE section in Chapter 6 of this Safety Guide.)

As Scaredy's party guest,
I agree with the above statements.

✗ ....Buddy................

Nothing makes party guests feel more welcome than a delicious snack table. As an exceptional host, you must go out of your way to tantalize their taste buds.

THE EERIE SNACK BAR:
(with cleverly cooked up, Halloween-themed finger foods)

Knuckle punch

Devilish eggs

Monster mash potatoes

Misfortune cookies

SandWitches

A SCAREDY TIP!
Dressing up to spook doesn't make you an ogre! Use a napkin and don't forget your manners!

HAIR-RAISING ACTIVITIES

Blow your guests away with Halloween fun that will leave them howling for more!

COSTUME CONTEST
(A classic competition for everyone)

WHAT'S TRICKY:
Not getting fingerprints on the trophy.

SNAKES AND LADDERS
(A creepy board game for the brave)

WHAT'S DAUNTING:
Playing the flute to hypnotize runaway snakes.

MOONWALK
(A lunatic, backward dance move for risk takers)

WHAT'S HORRIFYING:
Scuff marks on the floor.

A SCAREDY TIP!
Pipe organ music makes a great soundtrack for dancing. The very gloomy tempo will slow festivities down.

ZOMBIE BRAINTEASERS
(A puzzling IQ questionnaire for geniuses)

WHAT'S INTIMIDATING:
Everything.

Scaredy Squirrel's sure scared of skiing skeletons ...

TONGUE TWISTERS
(A mouthful for perfectionists)

WHAT'S THE CATCH:
Repeating 5 times while wearing vampire teeth.

GHOST STORIES
(A hallowed tradition for goosebump seekers)

WHAT'S SHOCKING:
Bookworms love them!

Once upon a time, in a faraway condo, there lived an evil witch with purple shoes.

On the 31st of October, or more precisely, on Halloween, she was cooking up a spell.

Suddenly, she noticed something terrifying!!! The yogurt had expired!

I JUST GOT CHILLS!

TELL ME ABOUT IT!

A SCAREDY TIP!

Remember to enjoy the festivities! Don't let unsigned paperwork or little monsters with a sweet tooth terrify you!

CHAPTER 8

IF ALL
ELSE FAILS ...

Playing Dead:

A survival technique perfected by Scaredy Squirrel.
This clever trick serves to confuse predators.
If calculations are correct, Frankenstein will first be puzzled, then try to think, and finally give up and spread terror elsewhere.
For optimal results, Playing Dead should be performed for 2 hours.
CAUTION! Never operate heavy machinery while Playing Dead.

Kids Can Press acknowledges the financial support of the Government of Ontario, through the Ontario Media Development Corporation's Ontario Book Initiative; the Ontario Arts Council; the Canada Council for the Arts; and the Government of Canada, through the CBF, for our publishing activity.

Published in Canada by
Kids Can Press Ltd.
25 Dockside Drive
Toronto, ON M5A 0B5

Published in the U.S. by
Kids Can Press Ltd.
2250 Military Road
Tonawanda, NY 14150

www.kidscanpress.com

The artwork in this book was rendered in charcoal pencil and Photoshop.
The text is set in Potato Cut.

Designed by Mélanie Watt

This book is smyth sewn casebound.
Manufactured in Tseung Kwan O, NT Hong Kong, China, in 4/2013 by Paramount Printing Co. Ltd.

Library and Archives Canada Cataloguing in Publication

Watt, Mélanie, 1975–
        Scaredy Squirrel prepares for Halloween : a safety guide for scaredies / written and illustrated by Mélanie Watt

ISBN 978-1-894786-87-4 (bound)

      I. Title.

PS8645.A8845286 2013   jC813'.6   C2013-901895-6

Kids Can Press is a Corus™ Entertainment company

For Eric and Julie

Special thanks to Debbie Rogosin.

HAPPY NON-THREATENING HALLOWEEN, EVERYONE!